WHEN THE
WIND BLOWS

Thomas Butler Feeney, S.J.

WHEN THE WIND BLOWS

A BOOK OF VERSES

By THOMAS BUTLER FEENEY, S.J.

DODD, MEAD & COMPANY · NEW YORK

1947

PRINTED IN THE UNITED STATES OF AMERICA
BY THE VAIL-BALLOU PRESS, INC., BINGHAMTON, N. Y.

To
TOM AND DELIA

Before amendations, many of these verses first appeared in *America, The Pylon,* and *From the Housetops.*

CONTENTS

Part I

Part II

xi

Part III

PART I

FAVORITES

"Which is your favorite doll?" I asked
  Of pretty Jane Marie.
"My old rag doll without any arms
  I'm fondest of," said she.

"And which of these kittens that play about
  Is the one you like the best?"
"Oh, the poor little thing without any ears
  I love above the rest . . .

"And of all the boys I know at school,
  The lad that I prefer
Is *you!*" she cried, and she skipped away
  Before I could answer her.

So I looked at the blear-eyed cat she chose,
  And the doll in faded pink;
Then I ran to the mirror and looked at me,
  And I tell you it made me think!

ORDER

My mother sent me to the store
At the corner of our street,
And when inside I looked around
At the goods piled high and neat:

Jars of jelly, quince and grape,
Cases of orangeade,
Kites and whips and garden tools,
Shovel and pick and spade,

Long rows of pies and marble cakes,
Raspberry-frosted squares,
Sweet pickles, peaches, nectarines,
Two-for-a-nickel pears,—

Then, into my gazing, the storeman said,
"Well, what can I do for you?"
And I answered, "A gallon of kerosene
And a bottle of furniture glue."

RED, WHITE AND BLUE

Grandpa Luke is dozing
Like a quiet autumn day
Full of frosty and of ruddy
Old remembrances of May.

But you just touch and wake him,
As we children often do,
To ask if our America
Is still red, white and blue,—

Then you will feel his fury
And a terror tear your heart
That a hundred million cannons,
Pointing at you, couldn't start,—

For a warm wind, slowly rising,
Seems to swell inside his veins
Where it turns to a tornado
Twirly-twisting in his brains,—

His brow's a breach of cloudheads,
Rains and lightnings are his eyes,
And his mouth a sea-pitched thunder
Madly tumbling in the skies.

When he thinks she doesn't love him
As they wander through the glow,
He swings the world above him
And the evening falls below.

Her feet turn into features
And her head becomes her feet
In the way that creeping creatures
Use a ceiling for a street.

He holds and presses on the skies
Of hilltop, valley, town . . .
Machines are sliding fireflies
That rollick upside down.

He chuckles at the crazy scene
He juggles for his mirth;
He balances a globe of green,
Boy Atlas of the earth.

His continent a lake of light,
The stars for yellow sands,
He dips his heels into the night
And walks upon his hands.

HALF-PINT

If you open your heart and open your mind
In a world that was made for you,
There's a bunch of marvelous things you'll find
Like a wonderful wish come true:

You can touch and feel the go and stop
Of the nails on a kitten's paws;
You can put your ear to a glass of pop
To hear the loud applause;

You can look at the wool on a lady's muff
That once was a Persian sheep;
You can look at a bottle of poison stuff
That's full of eternal sleep.

In my homework bag that's swelling
With the books my teacher loaned
Is a catechism telling
How a kingdom may be owned.

I learned that God is everywhere
Both in and out of school,
In the winding down of curls of hair
And the numbers on a rule.

And, stood in the corner for being bad,—
In a piece of looking-glass
Right in the palm of my hand I had
The prettiest girl in class.

FASTING

I read in a book that a holy saint
Would fast from food until he'd faint,
And fast from sleep until his eyes
Went blind from staring at the skies.

But chocolate-frosted, cream éclairs—
And running, two-by-two, up stairs—
And movie shows, and chewing gum . . .
These are the things I'm fasting from.

ALL SAINTS EVE

Halloo, halloo! for a Hallowe'en
In the crispy hail of the moon;
Apples piled like roses
On the crest of a cool lagoon.

The cider barrels yielding
Aroma sweet and strong;
Grape juice drips into a crock
Like a clock whose tick's a gong.

My mother steeping duck eggs
In phials liquid deep;
By the gold of the fire my father
Nods yes and no to sleep.

Powdered and flushed with fragrance
In an orange paper gown
My sister swishes out of doors
To a party in the town.

The kids are shouting in the lanes
For the mischief pranks they make;
Tomorrow, on my way to Mass,
I'll watch for the things they'll break.

But Pete and I must up to bed
After we read the prayers
In the holy book he won at school
For silence on the stairs.

The moon like a yellow pumpkin
Peeks through the windowpane;

I sleep, and he tires of peeking,
For when I wake again

He isn't there, but softly,
Outside, gay voices sigh.
My sister tiptoes to her room,
And, later, starts to cry;

Yet it is only the windmill
Squeaking in the wind.
I look over at Pete and he
With candle-dreams is blind.

I kiss his solemn, silly face,
And think of the fights we had;
I promise to be good to him,
Poor, nervous, cross-eyed lad.

I fall once more to slumber,
And over my slumber glow
Some of the saints I heard about
With nightgowns white as snow.

And one with a bright beard whispers,
Bending close to my face,
"Boy, O boy, are you loaded
With Sanctifying Grace."

IN THE DARK

Sitting trembling at my side
Marie was beautiful as a bride,
So I took her soft, moist hand in mine
And told her everything was fine.

With a quick release we began to move
Along a shiny, greasy groove
Into a shed that slid below
Where the air was wet and cool as snow.

My ardor turned to a shower of hail,
My spine to a column of ginger ale
When darkness took us by surprise
To clap his hands upon our eyes.

In a gradual pace we crawled on high
Into the clear expanse of sky,
Hearing the blare of distant bands
On the winking scapes of seas and lands.

And then, in a thunder of shrieks and yells,
We plunged to the heart of a hundred hells,
And lunged with the speed of the hounds of Mars
Through a dozen firmaments of stars.

We touched the poles of the heavens thrice
Where moons are flaming globes of ice,
Clearing the breadth of spheres that hum
In space that yearns to Elysium.

My body felt like a broken reed
When we strained at last to a slackened speed;

With a lurch we stopped, and I looked around
At my pitiful girl with her hair unbound,

Her face as blank and gray as lead,—
So I grabbed her arm, and I gulped and said,
"Let's try the merry-go-round, Marie,
One ride on that thing is enough for me."

BONAPARTE

From cloth of cotton to cloth of gold
To a shadowed print of trees
They change in the Corsican moonlight,
They stride on the Corsican breeze.

But tightly tethered by the waist
They sally forth in vain,—
And all night long the wind puts on
And takes them off again,

Until the boy Napoleon
Woke up feeling grand,
Rubbed his eyes, jumped out of bed,
Ran to the sill to stand

Looking through the window
And see the dawning shine
Over his clean blue rompers
Dancing on the line.

VOGUE

Now that I'm nine, I'm growing up,
And I need, before I'm old,
A king in silk of buttercup
Or a prince in mail of gold,

Someone who'll be a father
To seven pretty dolls,
Someone who'll help me gather
Minnows by waterfalls,

And someone who will tease me,
Or pull my flowing hair,
Or grab my wrist and squeeze me
Rough as a polar bear.

I must be clever or I'll die
Unwanted by an earl,—
So I'll snare a bright green butterfly
And stick it on a curl.

THE SECRET

One evening when the good Eileen
Put buttermilk to cool
Outside the kitchen door, she turned
And saw, to her delight,
A thousand stars and a silver moon
Reflected in the pool,
In the bucket of fresh-churned buttermilk
Set out beneath the night.

Dear Eileen was young in ways,
And wonder made her think
A show of jewels fair as this
Would never again befall;
So a fit of passion seized her
And in one unbroken drink
She downed the top of the buttermilk,
The moon, the stars and all.

Some people thought our lovely girl
Would never the least amount
To such a child of beauty
That she is, to their surprise;
But if they knew the secret
Then I think it might account
For the strange, sweet look of starlight
Ever beaming in her eyes.

Gwendolyn Donnelly studied in Milan,—
Mellowed in Italy's fruit-colored skies;
Pianoforte masters of Europe admitted
She played like an angel in alien guise.

Her début recital at Symphony Gardens
Attracted a crowd of a thousand or more;
The ripples of music that fell from her fingers
Set critics applauding as never before.

Sonatas and rhapsodies, waltzes, mazurkas,
And then a concerto in such a display—
She floundered in orchids and baskets of lilies . . .
It took twenty ushers to tote them away.

And yet I remember, when she was a baby,
Her first wee piano I bought in a shop;
It had only six notes for a scale, but she banged it
And banged till we thought that she never would stop.

And of all the pieces I heard at her concert,
Not one of them gave me emotions as sweet
As the sound of the tiny, ting-tong piano
She played, long ago, with her hands and her feet.

NAUGHTY GIRLS

THE EIGHTEEN NINETIES

Because her mother punished her
For being bold and proud,
Elaine ran up into her room
And whistled, right out loud.

THE NINETEEN TWENTIES

Because her mother told her twice
To mind her etiquette,
Marie put on a boy's attire
And smoked a cigarette.

THE NINETEEN FIFTIES

Because her mother frowned at her,
Clarice went raging mad,
She stole a jet-propulsion plane
And flew to Leningrad.

FOR A BIRTHDAY

The night never spindles
From shuttles of gold
The stars that I would
Your young eyes to behold.

Aurora may never
The violet brew
For dye of the blossoms
I'm bringing to you.

Twelve juicy jackets
Of sweet sherry snow
To touch to your lips
And to help you to grow.

A purple cool dozen,
The bloom of the south,
Bluebirds in a bundle
To fly to your mouth . . .

Sure, all the world's beauty,
By wishing it, comes
In a ninety cent specialty
Basket of plums.

VISION

Young Billy spent the most of his life where the lights flash
    on at five,
And Broadway and the avenues are luminously alive
With a million, billion bulbs that glow as the tons of granite
    rise
To cut the world from a single glimpse of dawn in the eve-
    ning skies,

For cigarettes and chewing gum in electrical displays,
Cologne, silk gowns and radios, theaters, cabarets,
Real beer in bottles of blue and gold and tires that blaze
    balloon
Make an advertising radiance out-glittering the moon.

But one night in September I took Billy by the hand
And I led him a hundred miles away to a far and fairy-land,
To a hill where not a house was built and not a soul was
    nigh,
And I gave him an undiluted look at night and the beaming
    sky—

The planets and all the satellites went by in a brilliant row,
The big and little dippers spilt their silvery, misty glow—
The Gemini, the Pleiades, Orion and the rest
Make myriad, magic gleamings on their saunter to the west;

While deep in the grass upon our backs we lay as still as
    death,
And I thought this wide magnificence had taken Billy's
    breath
Until I heard him whisper, with a quizzical look in his eyes,
"Say, what in the name o' holy hell are they tryin' to ad-
    vertise?"

He sat beside her on a hill;
The summer night was soft and blue;
Her rose-trimmed hat upon the grass
Was all there was between the two.

They both were shy about romance
And hadn't very much to say,
Until she broke the quietness
With childish thoughts, in her sweet way.

"Suppose," she said, "the stars fell down
Upon the fields in golden whirls,
I think you'd gather up your share
And give them all to other girls."

"I would, indeed, and none to you!"
He said to her immense surprise;
But quickly added, "They have need
Of stars who own no star-lit eyes."

And his fair words were like a moon
To lift the slow love-tide of her
Who set the rose-trimmed hat to bloom
Upon the other side of her.

AMERICAN REGAL

Princess in a purple gown,
Satin orchid for a crown,
Patters on the thoroughfare
In the city morning air.

Shoes of opal slender suède
Heeled as pointed as a blade,
Shoulders robed in summer fur,
Sheen of silk all over her.

Hair of auburn, set in curl,
Ring of topaz, brooch of pearl,
Hands like lilies on a stalk,
Face of primrose, and a walk

Beautifully poised with pride
Of a king's own chosen bride,
Shedding fragrance of a flower
On the golden early hour.

Greets the smiling corner cop,
Skips into a coffee shop,
Hangs her hat and mink away,
Dons a duster, takes a tray,

Sets the counters up with bowls
Of oranges and jelly-rolls;—
From the kitchen comes the shout,
"Good mornin', Mame!" the boss cries out.

LITTLE BERNICE

Little Bernice
Who watches geese
Along the mountainside,—
Little Bernice,
He'll never cease
To want you for his bride.
The silly drove that waddles by
Are swans upon a sea,
The crooked trees against the sky
Are lindens on a lea
Since little Bernice,
His joy, his peace,
Promised his love to be.

Little Bernice,
A golden fleece
Is on the mountain, now.
Little Bernice,
The stars increase
Above the mountain's brow.
The winds will blow the clouds about,
And many a goose will stray;
The winds will blow the twilight out
And all the dying day,—
But little Bernice,
His dream, his peace,
Will never blow away.

TWILIGHT

Into a rose-lamp store I goes
A fine rose-lamp to buy,
For we have a room that looks to the east,
My blind old man and I.

And though we have plenty of dawnings there
For me to talk about,
It's twilight folks has need of more
When youth has flickered out.

So into a rose-lamp store I goes,
In my mind a gorgeous plan
To take a sunset under my arm
Back home to my blind old man.

L. MARVIN GAMP

King Arthur's story made us glad,
Us two beneath her parlor lamp . . .
But gosh, I'm not Sir Galahad,
I'm plain L. Marvin Gamp.

Yet, since she told me I was he,
Each time I hike along a street
A sword is jangling side of me
And there are stirrups to my feet!

PEACOCK

Four ages loud with prayer, toil and pain
Have gone to rear the Venice that we know;
San Marco brightens like a jeweled vane
Where all the water alleys glide and glow.

Yet this pale man, this weaver here of rugs,
In half a year by hand and bended head,
Urged on by wine that's bought in gallon jugs,
Has plied the towered splendor into thread.

Within the palace close, the finished art
Upon a chamber's marble level set,
He slinks away, leaving behind his heart,
A secret city sleeping in a net.

Before the Prince, a youth of scanty wit,
Had glimpsed the gift, a peacock proud and tall,
Lured from the garden at the sight of it,
Spread a jealous tail of star plumes over all.

Just then His Highness came. With cluck and hiss
The peacock, rising, strutted through the door.
"Dear God!" the Doge exclaimed, "What bird is this
To lay an egg like Venice on my floor?"

THEODORA

She is a gift of God, and so
Of kindness she's in need
Who has a crowd of hungry ones,
In charity, to feed.

Think not she is unbeautiful
Whose beauty lies within,
For I heard a mission father say
Her soul is free from sin,—

And when it withers with her bones,
Let the village children vow
She's buttered many a crust of bread,
My one-horned cow.

THE POOL

There is a picture set in sand
And bordered by the dunes,
A window colored with tableaux
Of moving clouds and moons.

It is a pool in the desert
Under the glowing blue,
A burnished patch of water
The sun could not undo.

No beast or bird has seen it,
No wandering eyes looked where
No Arab maiden ever came
To twine her mirrored hair.

But night and day and dawning
In the wake of the skiey cars
Its lonely image gathers
Great gusts of flowers and stars.

MOONLIGHT

The moon is a trick of crystal panoply,
Under her fickle blooming, blind and dumb;

Yet, when the moon's a bow of mottled rose,
No earth can snare the red heart's eager drum;

Then worlds of green and blue are but a globe
Where, softly, dreams of a Nether Kingdom come.

BLUE

The bluebirds,
Gone to rest,
Will stir when dawn
Spills over their nest.

The bluebells,
Dark in the night,
Will wake when hills
Are gold with light.

But blue eyes
Will never start
From their slumbering
Upon my heart,—

Forever and ever
Asleep they'll stay
Till all blue stars
Are burned away.

And I wonder what
Young child could do
With shoes and a gown
Of baby blue.

Mon Dieu, how I miss her, ma mignonne Ivette,
Who played in the fields all day;
The sky was a picture bonnet of blue,
The clouds were tassels of gray.

A squirrel would come for the touch of her hand,
A dove for the perch of her head;
The butterflies thought that her mouth was a rose,
As bright as a rose is red.

She'd pluck a tall sunflower, and sway it to sleep,
And lay it to rest in a tree;
"Repose-toi là," she'd sing to a child
Impromptu melody.

Then once, of an evening, she followed the sun,
Thinking, no doubt, in the west
She'd find the place where a gold mother-bird
Hid her young stars in a nest.

Mon Dieu, how I miss her, ma mignonne Ivette
Who sleeps in the fields all day,
Under the pall of the violets
With her dream in the Great Far-away.

ARAB BOY

Tired of his playin'
With his cotton camel toy
And drowsy in the shadows
Is a baby Arab boy.

The fever's burnin' in him
And it's burnin' him away,—
He'll be goin' in the cool night
Before the dawn of day.

We must carry him in canvas
From the tent in which he dies
With the pale and secret slumber
Pressin' quiet on his eyes.

In the wastes of the arena
Where the soft and sifted flows
Of the white dust of the desert
Sweep in dry and dreamy rows,

We will put to bed forever
Sleepy child and sleepy toy,—
For the sandman's comin'
To a baby Arab boy.

AMELITA

Amelita tends a fruit store
On Investment Square,
And many a banker, going home,
Has bought provisions there.

Her wealth of charm allures the hearts
That work at wealth all day;
And when she smiles, the plums and pears
Bring back their groves of May.

She is all innocent and kind,
A child of tenderness,
A cool repose for gentlemen
Tired of their own success.

To purchase grapes and oranges
You wonder if they came,
Or just to stand and look at her,
And speak her pretty name!

But cherry lips are not for sale,
Nor brambleberry eyes,
And the peaches blooming in her cheeks
No banker ever buys.

THE BEAUTY OF HER FACE

We met when August meets July,
Where lavender lines-off the lanes,
And instantly he stormed my soul
With young love's ecstasies and pains.

He was so cool and debonair
Against the green and azured heat;
I was so girlish and so sure
I was incomparably sweet.

But, some days later, as we sat
In a garden trysting place,
He turned, as she was passing by,
And saw the beauty of her face.

He saw the beauty of her face
No man could ever look upon
Without thinking of a sun
That golden on a midnight shone.

Then the glory of the afternoon,
Hot with fragrant, purple flower,
Struck a sudden veil of chill
On my shoulders and the hour.

The ardent notes of songs he sang,
Seeming to sing them just for me,
Broke like icicles that fall
On the blue sill of a sea.

The tender, eager words he said,
The first that I had ever known,

Surged and circled from my heart
To the very depth of bone.

The diamond clearing of the air,
The summer's meaning and reward,
A dwelling built of sacrament
Guarding its guerdon with a sword, . . .

All these, and a thousand moonlit dreams
That hope speeds higher than the skies,
Were touched and tumbled into mist
When he looked up and saw her eyes.

SAYING IT WITH FLOWERS

He handed her a bright bouquet
As ads and pictures told him to,
And saw her secret heart betray
Her love in flowers, red and blue.

For, off her guard, she heard him speak
His rival's name, "Nathaniel Wise,"
When a rose came blushing to her cheek
And glories opened in her eyes.

If you are over twenty, you may dream a dream forever
In the chambers of the flower-bordered night,
But you will never know again, not once again forever,
The young heart's, the deep heart's, the wild heart's delight;

The crystal music of the world may break your heart for-
    ever,
Or beauty gush against your eyes when early moons are
    fair, . . .
But you may never crush again your lips upon white won-
    der,
The blue stars bursting in your blood, the red wind in your
    hair!

COCKTAIL

At midnight, in among his flocks
Of bottled big and little cocks,
Malfatti stands behind the bar,
His arms a fold, his eyes a star
That shines on all that he has done
With liquid bantams, one by one.

From sly experience of years
Malfatti knows his chanticleers
Become like those who take them in
And are not what they might have been;
For all may laugh and all may play,
But only the innocent are gay.

And even then they change again
To birds of bliss or birds of pain, . . .
Ah, well the old Malfatti knows
That scarlet roosters turn to crows,—
But the white cocks with the white tails
Tomorrow will be nightingales.

Will anyone explain it, please,
How love, that weighed him to his knees
With a burden of wild ecstasies,
Was rid of with such quiet ease?
Or how, as slowly as it came,
It thinned out into something tame;
Until, with nine days' wonder gone,
His heart is vacant as a stone . . .
As peaceful as when, long ago,
A silent boy trudged home alone
Through the driving rain or the driving snow,
Glad to have been the only fool
Who *went* to find there was no school?

U.S. MAIL

Tip of my pen
On scented blue,
Once again
I'm writing you.

Once again
The dark ink strives
To mend the patches
Of our lives.

O words, be clear!
And words be strong
To carry love
And a love song!

The tune be sweet
To your sweet eyes,
And, if you're foolish,
Make you wise.

If I be stubborn,
Make me mild,
Sincere and humble
As a child.

Lines be brilliant,
Fraught with grace
Our dull division
To retrace.

Bring bliss and pleasure
Out of pawn!

Turn up the flowers,
Light the dawn!

Wake again
The vacant sea!
Build a vanished
World for me!

To give me life,
To give me breath
After the blight
Of slow death,

To make a heaven
Out of hell,—
O ink, be brave
My heart to tell!

THE BERRY PICKERS

Into the hours, into the sun
The berry pickers go;
And some like laughing children run
To wake the valley lanes with fun,
All eager till the work be done . . .
But some are slow.

For some must toil with heavy hands
To push the thorns apart,
To clear the berry-covered lands,
In dreary groups, in weary bands
Who've learned that no one understands
A weary heart.

O aching finger tips that bled
Where the long light falls, . . .
Beside the cruel, spiny bed
I've listened, and the torn wind said
Why berry boxes burn so red
In the market stalls.

WRECK

The night is on the sea,
The stars are on the waves,
The ships are anchored low
In cool and finny graves.

The ships are broken toys
The wind and billows tore,
The mariners are dolls
Upon a coral floor.

The night is on the waves,
The dark on level spars—
The stars are on the sea,
The ships are in the stars.

ARAN LULLABY

La, la, loo,
What am I to do,
Close your eyes and go to sleep, my baby.

La, la, lay,
Night will pass away,
Close your eyes and go to sleep, my baby.

Someone whom we love, dear,
Is sleeping in the sea,
Someone who will never come
Again to you and me.

La, la, low,
You're too young to know,
So close your eyes and go to sleep, my baby.

GARDEN REQUIEM

Here, where the concert leader lies
More hushed than muted sound,
Old melodies in blossoms flow
When rhythm buds of jasmine blow.
Chromatic movement petals play;
Cadenzas rise on speedwell spray.
A scherzo leaps in broken lines
Of yellow furze and eglantines,
While grace notes of the butterflies
Go fluting from the ground.

TWO DEAD ROSES

One was a weeshy rose, one was a queen.
One was a poor thing, sad to be seen;
One was as lovely as light on the green.

The weeshy rose had such a small way to go
To come to the death that the roses know:
A simple fall, a step or so
From the top of the stem to the grave below.
I loved and pitied the weeshy one,
And we both found rest when her days were done.

But the beautiful had such a long way to go,
Across the mountains and through the snow
And over the seas where the cold winds blow,
To come to the death that the roses know!
I seemed not to care for her, lovely apart;
Now that she's dead she troubles my heart.

Maybe it's silly, or maybe it's sound,—
Anyhow, look at them—dust on the ground.

THE COMFORTER

Once, when a lady was lonely
For love to come again,
Her lips were big with sadness
And her eyes were bright with pain.

She thought about tomorrow
And would it bring relief;—
Tomorrow came but just the same
Her heart was hurt with grief.

She cried, at last, for comfort
From someone mournful too,—
And, suddenly, beside her saw
Your loneliness and you.

THEME WITH VARIATIONS

Praise be to God for petty woes
That somebody sees or nobody knows,
For straight hair or sore toes . . .
And a dull gray sky in the morning—

For favorite fountain pens that leak,
For *café noir* that is too weak,
For overcoats that aren't warm,
For syllogisms out of form . . .
And a dull gray sky in the morning—

For cheeks aflame with too much rouge,
For villages that are not Bruges,
For a grand piano not in tune,
For a Mardi Gras with an absent moon . . .
And a dull gray sky in the morning—

For the spun top that will not hum,
For chairs alive with chewing gum,
For the sleeping bird that will not wake,
For too many lights on a birthday cake . . .
And a dull gray sky in the morning—

Praise be to God for petty woes
That all surmise or few suppose,
For a lonely heart or a cold nose . . .
And a dull gray sky in the morning.

PART II

CAPTAIN KELLY LETS HIS DAUGHTER
GO TO BE A NUN

Tiffany, Tiffany,
What are you doing
Deep in the mines
And under the sea?
Come out of that, Tiffany,
Out of the caverns,
Out of the ocean
And listen to me!

I own a jewel
Blanche as the moonlight,
Pearl as a sunset
Star on a hill;
Billions of bullion
Never could buy her,
Only the Gold
Who is God ever will.

Don't dilly-dally all the day,
Shy Genevieve, run off to play!
Call out the pretty collie pups,
And skip among the buttercups.

The flowers spread their cloaks for you
To sit and gaze at cloud and blue,
The green of treetops waving shade
And all the colors Love has made.

Be done with chores of house and farm,—
There's corn-meal on your dimpled arm,
Dish-water stains your muslin dress
And all your curls are in a mess.

Don't fuss or bother any more,
Shy Genevieve, come through the door!
The dogs are yelping,—in the sky
Go pale armadas blooming by.

TEA AT DELPHI

When Margaret finished her cup of tea
She showed the empty cup to me
Inside of which the tea leaves made
A pattern delicate as shade
Where Margaret asked me to divine
A picture hid in the small design.

So, turning the teacup handle down,
I traced a nun in a robe of brown . . .
And Margaret's merry eyes of blue
Grew deep with a rush of velvet rue,
And all of the glittering rings and bands
For a moment fell from her arms and hands
While the kettle, steaming, wove in air
A hint of veils about her hair,
And a cloud of angels, seething white,
Went over her face in a web of light
That made her loveliness transpose
To a dearest Margaret of the snows . . .

But, seeing her lover stare at me,
She asked for another cup of tea.

THE IMAGE

Slender, subtle, beautiful,
Blithe in evening as a fawn,
She walked, a clad-in-silver dream
Of star-gleam upon the lawn.

So tenderly her girlish soul
Informed her body, toe to hair,
One could have known the yearning spent,
At last content that she was fair.

Yet never until she's won to death
Shall she surmise what Love has done
That, wrought of splendor, she might go
Along the glow of the setting sun.

Oh, listen at the looking-glass
To hear the singing in your eyes,
"His Heart, ableeding on the plain,
From pain of unrequital . . . dies!"

CHOOSEY SUZIE

Oh, some of the girls that I know
Are easily satisfied,
They'd marry anybody
That their silly eyes have spied;
But the kind of a man that I'd love
Has got to have eyes of blue,—
Or maybe deep and dark eyes,
Or hazel eyes would do.

Oh, some of the girls that I know
Most anyone would wed,
But my man must have blond hair,
Or chestnut hair, or red;
He's got to be big and handsome,
If not, then slim and tall,—
Or maybe fair to middling,
Or maybe plain and small.

Oh, the kind of a man that I'd love
Must be a wealthy lad,
Or one who, if he had it,
Would give me what he had;
He's got to be good at dancing,
Graceful, neat and grand,—
And yet I'm sure I'd take him
Though he could hardly stand.

Dear Joseph, spouse of Mary,
You are a saint, and so
There's no use telling you a lie
For well I know you know

My days are drab and dreary,
Send someone soon along
To put a lilt into the tune
Of my life's dull song.

If a gentleman should read this,
Discovering what is true,
Here is what I ask him:
How about you?

KATY'S LITANY

Sacred Heart of Jesus,
Font of life and grace,
Guide the lost and lonely
Of the human race.

Heart the Holy Spirit
Formed in Mary's womb,
Have mercy on the dear ones
Sleeping in the tomb.

Heart of tender pity
Grief-and-sorrow-tossed,
Let me find the silver
Earrings that I lost.

Ease this old arthritis
That's munching at my bones;
Stop Marie from trying
To keep up with the Jones.

Heart the deep desire
Of the everlasting hills,
Induce the girls to give me
Enough to meet the bills.

Comfort of the dying,
Delight of all the saints,
Allow me always near to
Our Julie when she faints.

Strength of those in trouble,
Temptation, want or pain,

Bring my bad boy Roger
Home to my arms again.

Help Mr. Moore and family
To hire a decent flat,
One that's near the car barns
Where he's working at.

With praise and great thanksgiving
For the good You've done and do,
Most Sacred Heart of Jesus
May all Your dreams come true.

WOMAN WANDERER

Through stones and mire of the lonely road I wander along
    alone,
Searching and seeking for someone I've known, or have
    never known;
I cannot remember if he was tall, if he was big or he was
    small,—
I cannot remember if his eyes were brown or his hair brown,
So I wander along alone seeking him from town to town,
And I look at you, and you, and you
To see if you or you will do,—
But I never mind him,
And I never find him.

The children hush as they pass me by
And run away from the look in my eye.

I cannot remember if he was my father or my brother,
Or if I was his bride or his mother,
But my heart is wanting him so I go
In my tattered dress of calico
And my torn shoes through the winds from the skies,
And the gray hair blows into the tears in my eyes,
Yet I never cry and I never smile
As I wander along alone seeking him mile on mile,
And I never mind him,
And I never find him.

Ah well, I know that God is true,
And one day, please Him, the want and the pain,
The storm and the rain,
In the clouds of my brain
Will break into blue.

And I'll find him, I'll find him, my lost love,
And we will never part,
I'll keep him forever and ever,
His heart against my heart.
God will gather me far away
To the Kingdom of Music and Gold,
Make me a Princess beautiful
For all the world to behold,
And my wandering life be a legend
Never again to be told.

BETWEEN MY HANDS

Between my hands I hold a head
So silky soft with curls of brown,
A golden globe of miracles
Surpassing ocean, field or town.
What storms of wonder . . . spinning dreams
Of magic mountains, lakes and lands,
Of thrones and kingdoms, dolls and God,
I hold between my very hands!

Sweet face uplifted to my face,
And eyes that hurl against my eyes
More art than yet flares on the earth
From fires of our lost paradise,
For one limp moment, wild with love,
I would my name were sudden death
That I might slay your fragile pulse
And gather off your latest breath
Before the winter of the world
Can break the lilies of your soul
And Christ, Our Lord, pay all His Blood
To make you whole, to make you whole.

ALL HALLOWS

Choirs of saints look down this night
On little-girl eyes of blue
That meekly, sadly, shadow-bright
Are looking up at you.

Francis, Joseph, John and Mark,
Come back to earth again!
Shed golden guarding on the dark
Of her small night of pain.

Theresa, Margaret and Joan,
Into your keeping take
This aching burden, lest alone
She grieve and her heart break.

Hallowed be this trembling dove
Ever and ever the same,
And He who wounds her for His Love,
Hallowed be His Name.

THE CHOSEN ONE

Marie had called him, "Precious clown,"
"Sweet lark," "More lovable than wise,"
Until she caught a glimpse of tall
Lit candles in his eyes.

Their flame made all her heart afraid;—
She blew at them her beauty's breath,
Not knowing why the sun and stars
Will throb and burn to death.

And when he went the lone white way
That storms the hills of Paradise,
Marie searched well each lover's look
For candles in his eyes.

The altar looked from golden eyes
And wept with silent, slow surprise,
Wondering who could be to blame
That no priest came.

The candles, whispering softly, died;
The cruet wine and water dried;
Some quiet children, kneeling there,
Grown tired of waiting, tired of prayer,
Arose and, genuflecting, went
Into the dark, and were content.

Then, drop by drop, the voided room
Fell dull and dreamless as a tomb.
On wings of wind a whimpering moan
Came up and kissed the altar stone;
And once, and once (it was not well),
A brown rat struck the silver bell.

So now from dry and sightless eyes
The altar gapes with no surprise
Through age on age by worlds and suns,—
Oh let us pray, forsaken ones,
For him or her who was to blame
That no priest came.

THE LONELY MAN

(FOR BOYS IN A SUNDAY SCHOOL)

The lonely man awoke at night
To light a cigarette;
He heard a belfry iron out
The hour the dark will set.

Slippered, bathrobed, cushioned up,
He clicked a rose light on
That uttered flowers like a very,
Very meager dawn.

For that the yellow drug he took
Gave no release of sleep,
For that he was all, all alone,
He started in to weep.

He wept for John and Marjorie,
For Harriet, Jane and Joe . . .
Five memories to be filled with tears
Ranged in a dream of row.

He wished he, too, were dead and gone
And buried in the Styx . . .
What else could he wish, poor man, because
He had no Crucifix.

And if Christ did not die for you
Though brave, as brave you are,
Your courage would go out at last
And not shine like a star.

Make no mistake: unbending, true
And fierce is the pain of loss!
So, everybody stand up, now,
And make the Sign of the Cross!

LA BOHÊME

Mistress Bohemian buckled her gown,
Straightened her stockings and skipped into town.
Her coat was a fox and her mouth was a rose—
But what she was thinking of nobody knows.

She flung me a glance with what might have been eyes
If they weren't so dark and they weren't so wise—
Then doing the thing that a gentleman must,
I lowered my gaze to a pavement of dust.

When I looked up she had melted away
Into eternity, into the day—
Walking as prettily, walking as proud
As a bird who can conquer the breeze and the cloud.

I fumbled the journal I held in my hand
And the dime I would pay for a ride on the land,
Keeping in conscience the look that she gave
Which grew, upon pondering, questioning—grave.

I stood on a corner of Washington Square
And knew it was Christ, not I, who was there—
Christ of the lonely ones, Christ of the weak—
And I groaned in my heart for the one I would seek:

"Flower bird flying on seas without goal,
Come back with your body and bring me your soul!
Your red mouth is hung like a lamp in my mind—"
But the cry of her eyes was lost on the wind.

I know there are many who doubt me,
But, when with the sleeping I lie,
Let them say this much about me:
For love of my Love I would die.

It seems that a name will not find me,
For dark is the light in the sky;
Through nights of the shadows that blind me:
For love of my Love I would die.

The coward that seeks me may woo me
And win me to him with a sigh;—
In grief for the sins that undo me:
For love of my Love I would die.

So silly a going may take me
As poison from eating a pie;
Though the glory of martyrs forsake me:
For love of my Love I would die.

And if I should go young tomorrow,
Or old in a far by-and-by,
Remember, to comfort your sorrow:
For love of my Love I would die.

Or if you should come where I'm sleeping
And stand with a tear in your eye,
Remember, to comfort your weeping:
For love of my Love I would die.

WHAT IS DEATH?

Death is the going cold of a feeble fire;
The fall of silver snow.
Death is the unknown ocean of desire
Where all floods flow.

Death is the flying-out of brilliant birds
When silent gongs are rung.
Death is the perfect melody of words
No heart has ever sung.

Death is a white young face against your face,
A soft breath to your breath.
The hushing-up of shadow-blighted space
Is firm, gray death.

Death is the taking off of wrinkled shoes,
The sandaling on of flame.
Death is the loss of all you would not lose
For love or wild fame.

Death is a voice of flutes from off the sun
That calls by sea and land . . .
You leave the supper dishes half undone,
And go, and understand.

A clock will dimly chime, a candle light,
And, bending by your bed,
May Jesu give your lips a sweet "Good-night!"
When you, dear child, are dead.

THE SISSY

When Jesus comes to judge me
The minute that I die,
My lips will start to quiver,
I'll bow my head and cry.

When He names the ten commandments
And the eight beatitudes,
I'll just stand there without a word
In one of my bawling moods.

Then He'll pause to look me up and down
From crumpled hair to toes,
He'll see the cast in my left eye
And the scar across my nose.

And He'll take my head against His Heart,
His Arms around my throat,
And press so hard my face will feel
The buttons on His coat.

THE FAR LULLABY

Twi-light falling
Night birds calling,
Now's the time to lull a baby sleeping;
But I'm only
Sad and lonely,
God has taken mine into His keeping.

Yet will I sing a far lullaby
I sang when my baby was near me—
Lull lullaby, off to the sky, . . .
Tell me, my love, that you hear me!

Twi-light falling
Night birds calling,
All the silver lights of Heaven gleaming;
Stars are welling,
Softly telling,
Telling that you're safe and sweetly dreaming.

BRIDEGROOM

She put her slippers in the shoe press,
Put her garments each away,
Washed and dried, and brushed her hair,
And went to sleep until the day.

She always knew that she might die
In dream, and one must find her so
Prim and proper, bright and fair,
Glad heart to the last aglow.

Thus we found her of a morning,
Satin-smooth in perfect place
Gown and coverlets and curls,
And the hush in her sweet face.

She was so darling, do not blame Him,
He who took His bride to be
And with all her love went flying
Like a wind across the sea.

FOR INSTANCE

Just take, for instance, Billy Brown,
The best prize-fighter in our town;
He wasn't dapper, he wasn't bland,
He had no polish and no land.

He married pretty Helen Snow;
Like Juliette and Romeo,
They lived as lovebirds in a tree,
And they were as happy as they could be.

Then when she died, some two years back,
He stood above her, dressed in black,
And wept, his heart cut clean in two,—
A beautiful thing for a man to do.

And, every morning since, you'd find
Him kneeling there among his kind,
Going to early Mass to pray
For his loved one who has passed away.

No doubt, in the Body of his Lord,
Marked with thorn and spike and sword,
He found a purpose for the toll
That pain was taking of his soul.

When war broke out, he swiftly went
To service as to sacrament;
And when he fell in action, peace
Came with a Heaven of release.

His last brief letter said that he
Would find her in Eternity,—

O rare in the world, in court or mart,
The tribute of the faithful heart!

Nobody knows why little girls
Marry marquises and earls;
Maybe, my darling, it's because
They still believe in Santa Claus.

MIDSUMMER BY THE SEA

The cloudless night reels off translucent showers,
A star is caught in every treetop plume,
The ocean rolls and swells like molten silver,—
My sight and sense are shadowed in a tomb.

I sit and read a book that tells how Heaven
Is, as the pictured lights upon the sea,
Mirrored in what the wide earth keeps of beauty,—
In her child-holiness God came to me.

Above their teacups, near-by guests are saying
Some fragrant thoughts whose pleasure has to do
With what the soft, pine-scented winds are telling,—
Her mouth was sweet, her eyes were glad and blue.

This hour of dreams the world's a gleaming garden
With veils of blossoms sifted on the ground;
A distant band begins to play a love waltz
And the beaming bell of sky rings gay with sound.

Almighty God, I thank You for this moment,
For flowers of moonlight walking on the wave,—
But she had such small hands to take my heart in,
She holds it bound beside her in the grave.

What a sad and secret sound is a good-bye
Changing from word to water in the eye,
Troubling the heart one loves to a bitter cry:

Good-bye is like a broken china doll
Whose hundred pieces each is integral,
A puzzle on the floor from crib to wall,—

Is like the dearest, shining-golden fish
Found floating dead inside a global dish,
A home supplied with all that it could wish,—

Is like the curled and dusty-brown repose
That settles deadlier than winter snows
And strikes with gradual lightning on the rose.

Good-bye is a child whose yearning wants release,
Who wanders off to a far land seeking peace,
And finds a deeper loneliness increase,—

Is the quiet-coming, autumn cold that falls
On someone grown too old for festivals
Whose evening gowns are changing into shawls,—

Is the dusky-purple, sunset hush that blooms
When clouds go out in all the azure rooms
And mountains wear the mantle of the glooms.

Our Father knows all this full well, and so
He calls us, one by one, from here below,—
And, one by one, we answer His hello.

SING NO MORE OF LOVE

This is the ultimate love song
A man ever sung:
"Your eyes no more ring out my heart
As a bell is rung;
The last bright rose from off your lip
Has blown away;
Gone is the golden bride I won
On a wedding day.

Your mind of my delight is lost
In a well of fears;
You've gone in age beyond me, now,
By years and years,
But I clasp and kiss and keep you, dream,
In groan and grieve,—
O God the Weaver, God the Wool
And God the Weave!"

DIALOGUE

"Good morning, sir," said Joachim;
"Good morning, sir," said I to him.
"And how does the infant Mary be?"
"The queen of baby girls," said he.

"She's off to sleep at candlelight
And never bothers us at night;
Always as happy as a rose—
She'll be a wonder when she grows."

"Well, hardly marvel people can
That such a child should come to Anne."
"It's true for you!" said Joachim.
And then, "Good day!" said I to him.

SAINT ANNE'S DAUGHTER

"Snow-bright Lady Girl, where have you been,
You look so troubled, so pale and so thin?
What has become of my daughter's eyes,
So secret and beautiful now, and so wise?

"Moon-white Innocence, where have you flown?
Say you've not left me or I'll be alone!
Come to me, darling, and tell me your woe
And I'll be your mother whatever I know."

"Mother, my mother, oh, never!
I'm your White Innocence ever.
The Wind and the Flame and the Wings of a Dove
Have sought me and found me and filled me with Love.

"My eyes are the Morning Star, my lips the Rose,
My arms are a Garden where the lonely repose;
The bright Gates of Heaven have opened apart
And God is a Baby sleeping under my heart."

THE GIFT

"Lady Mary, where are you going
Out of Nazareth Town?
It's late in the day
To journey away,
And the bridge, they say, is down."

"I must be going to Bethlehem,"
The Lady Mary said,
Folding a shawl
To cover her all
And over her small brown head.

"And will you bring us a present home
From the land you travel to,
A big surprise,
Like a doll whose eyes
Are beautiful, wise and blue?"

"I will bring you a Doll of Gold,"
Sweet Lady Mary smiled
And waved farewell,
As a silence fell
On the wondering spell of a child.

CHRISTMAS GUIDE

I

Lamps that burn at Christmas,
Flame a golden way
Lest the shades of evening
Lead us all astray.

Stars that shine at Christmas,
Fire the silver snow,
Show us in the glooming
Where we ought to go.

Eyes alight at Christmas,
Two searching Baby Eyes,
In your secret shadow
Dreams our Paradise.
La, la, lo,
When we find You so,
We will love and hold You
Warm in a world of woe.

II

Bells that sound at Christmas,
Calling from afar,
We will soon be coming,
Coming where you are.

Birds that sing at Christmas,
Birds of a winter night,
Fly and sing above us,
Guide our steps aright.

Eyes that call at Christmas,
Two seeking Eyes Divine,
Every word You're calling
Tells us, "You are Mine!"
La, la, lo,
When we find You so,
You will make us merry
All in a world of woe.

SONG WIT WOIDS

I ups and goes to midnight Mass on Christmas,
Though I hadn't went to Mass for 'leven years.
I remembered me baby sister who's gone wrong as bad as
    me,
And down came de tears.

I thought o' what saps we are to fall for de woild's baloney,
I felt humility, and I took a sock at me pride;
I felt like a plug kneelin' in choich, I felt like a rat in a rain-
    bow,
I felt like a flea on a bride.

It wasn't de music, it wasn't de lights and de roses,
Nor de swell lookin' goils goin' to Holy Communin what
    took me down . . .
But it was de crib wit a wooden stature of de Blessed
    Voigin
In her blue gown.

I wisht to God I was a kid again up in de Bronx
So dat she could take me in her arms at midnight Mass;
I felt like crawlin' through de hay to be there beside her
And take de place of de ass.

Wasn't He sweet! Wasn't He sweet!
There was pins and needles in my feet
From kneeling long in the frosty stall,
But I never minded the pain at all.

Wasn't she nice! Wasn't she nice!
His darling mother who kissed us twice!
And the angels with their gowns of rose,
Were they truly real, do you suppose?

Let's hurry, Jane! Let's hurry, Jane!
We'll ask our mothers to go again!
We'll bring some candles, some fuel-sod
And a baby goose for the Son of God.

SONG OF LITTLE

A little girl, a little shed,
A little town, a cattle stall,
A little straw, a little bed,
A little Child—that is all
That can be said
About the Little Light, the Flame
That into the dark world came.

So if you're little, if you're small,
If nobody cares for you at all,
If, through the darkness in and out,
You, lonely laden, go about,
Your heart is ready, your heart is right
And little enough for the Little Light
Of Christmas night—
And little enough for the Little Flame
That into the sad world came.

GOLD

Once on the very first
Christmas morn,
As angels gathered
By the moon's white horn,
God was a Baby
When God was born.

God was as easy
For your arms to fold
As any small infant
Three hours old,—
And to take Him was to have
All a world of gold.

MITCHA, THE WRESTLER

(A LEGEND)

Mitcha, the wrestler, six feet four,
Who rocks the walls and warps the floor
Whenever he ambles the hall along—
Set out to hear the angel song.

Mitcha, the mountain, whose arms are guards
That can hurl a man a dozen yards,
Went thundering down to Bethlehem—
And the Powers took him for one of them.

Mitcha, the great, with a face that's bent,
With a chest as solid as cold cement,
Gave up the lasses, the beer, the mirth—
And came to find the Light of earth.

He found the Infant God the Son,
He gave Him the diamond belt he won,
He knelt him down to say a prayer—
And the bulls in the stall began to stare.

And then, for all of us to see,
He sat him down on Our Lady's knee,
For though she was just a slender girl
With her still child eyes and her hair in curl,

"She is my mother," the Mitcha said
As he pressed his proud and mighty head
Against Our Lady's loving heart—
And felt his own one break apart.

87

And all of a sudden the Mitcha grew
As small as ever his either shoe,
As small as a newborn baby boy—
And Our Lady sang him a song of joy.

Our Lady sang him a song of rest
When he fell asleep on Our Lady's breast;
We watched him fade and we watched him dim,—
And that was the last that we saw of him.

SAINT JOSEPH MINDS OUR LORD

Holy Baby not mine,
Go to sleep and close your dark-sweet, your mother's eyes.
Holy Baby Divine,
When your mother comes home, if she'll find you safely
    sleeping, she'll be filled with a glad surprise.

When your tiny hand, so softly twining,
Holds my fingers,—God holds my fingers;
When your infant gaze looks on a sifted sunbeam shining,—
Sun on sun lingers.
When you weep God is weeping,
And when you sleep God is sleeping.

Holy Baby not mine,
Close your dark-sweet eyes and let them thus remain.
Holy Baby Divine,
When your mother comes home to find you safely sleeping,
    maybe she'll let us two be all alone together again.

NIGHT AFTER CHRISTMAS

We eat in the kitchen once again,
A dreary, hurried sup.
I gulp the tea that's weak and cool,
Served in the usual cup.

Since Jane Marie and her family
Have gone back home to town
It's lonely in the lighted room,
And the Christmas blooms are brown.

The glittering tree is not so nice
Without the candy canes.
Some of the colored bulbs are dead
In the candled windowpanes.

My woolly lamb has lost its wheels,
The rocking horse won't swing,
The clown that used to somersault
Won't wind or anything.

The toy crib lost the ox it had,
The hay, the star, the snow,—
And the Baby Jesus lies alone
Under the radio.

SONG OF EGYPT

O Rose! The sweetest, nicest boy
Came over to play with me—
His curls were dark, his eyes were bright
And beautiful to see.

We talked about such grown-up things
While resting in the shade
Beside the glowing poppy patch
That you and I had made.

He told me how the flower stars
Could grow without a stem—
He knew them all so well you'd think
He really planted them;

And Oh—the ruby ring I lost
About a year ago—
He found it for me quick as light
Down by the barley row.

You know the darling boy I mean,
He can't be more than four—
His father is that Jewish man
Who fixed the hen-house door.

God made a rocket full of gold . . .
He touched it with a flare . . .
Soaring, it coiled a trailing fire
That melted in the air.

The risen bolt in thunder burst,
Scattering worlds of stars,
A spray of constellations
Like a blast of silver spars.

All these, as rocket lights will do,
Were riding on to die,
When God said, "Stop!" . . . And there they are,
Still shining in the sky.

ITEM

Look at the fireflies flick in the trees,
The glowworms gleam in the flowers,
The flash of the phosphorous fish in the seas,
The rainbow shine in the showers!

Think of the power of that lamp of a moon
And the star globes burning by!
Or reckon the strength of the sun at noon
That lightens the world and the sky!

Imagine the heat that can scatter the chill
Of the ocean, the air and the ground!
Dear God, what a bill! Your Heart'll stand still
When the first of the month comes around!

There'll come a time when God will say,
"Be all my sunlight furled!
Take down the sky, I'll stage no more
The pageant of the world!

"Let all the blazing star balloons
Go floating off in space!
Close down the moon's bright parasol
And pack it in the case.

"My winged acrobats are tired
From whirling in the air,
And all my animals must rest—
The elephant, the bear,

"My well-trained dogs and honeybees,
My lions in their caves,
My glossy seals that, twisting, dive
In depths of the freezing waves,

"Sardines and whales performing
To the roll of the ocean drums
Where seven seas are seven rings
Of salt aquariums,

"The traveling cribs of kangaroos,
My horses, dray or prize,
The fennec listening all with ears,
The cuscus all with eyes,

"The zebra, the rhinoceros,
The lyrebird, the roe

Must now forever cease to be
A part in any show.

"The silver hail and snow effects,
The thunder tumbling loud,
The tug of war in turning tides,
The clouds on crimson cloud,

"The concert of the storms and winds,
The tapestry of bowers,
The tragedy of twilights,
The festivals of flowers—"

Yes, there will come, most certainly,
A time when God will say,
"Be still, ye wonders of the night
And wonders of the day!

"Let fall the sky, fold up the earth
And pull the long poles down,
For after a run of a million years
The circus is leaving town!"

Surely fun will flourish
When the present world is past,
In a life where last is first,
And the first, last.

A mouse will lead
A panther pack
Around the disk
Of the zodiac.

The lark will hark
To the sparrow's bid;
The peacock do
As the violet did.

An egg will hatch
A golden goose;
A castle cradle
A papoose.

A leopard like
A lamb will curl
Up on the lap
Of a baby girl.

Aser, the barber,
Will be the beau
The débutantes
Will want to know;

Dowdy Nora
The belle brunette
Of the perfume ads
In a gay gazette.

The duke will polish
The butler's boots,
The duchess mend
His union suits.

The dog will tease the flea,
The corn will peck the crow,
The canary plague the kitten,
And the lion flee the doe.

The time will tell the clock,
The weather tell the vane,
The dawn proclaim the rooster,
And the herring eat the crane.

The swan will soar the mountains,
The eagle swim the seas,
The busy, buzzing poppy
Plunder honey from the bees;

The Private pin a medal
On the President's lapel;
The Apostle tell the Atheist
To go to hell.

The drake will hunt the fox,
And the fox, the hound;
The sword be stabbed,
And the lake, drowned.

All verse will shine
With beautiful words—
And the nest fly home
To the birds.

97

TWO-SONG CHARLIE

I

They call me Two-song Charlie,
And I own, without ado,
Like Ruth among the barley,
My songs are only two.

I always sing them *soli*,
Twin works of classical fame:
"Mother Machree" and "Holy
God We Praise Thy Name."

I've sung for the Catholic Daughters
And other groups of note;
I've sung on Atlantic waters
At a concert on a boat.

"Mother Machree" got great applaud
At a wedding or a shower;
And once I sang the "Holy God"
In church at the Holy Hour.

As young as four and twenty
I used to make them cry;
I've seen, while singing, plenty
Of tears in many an eye.

I start with a *moderato*,
The tone with a fervor swells;
I turn on the old *rubato*
And it sighs like a chime of bells.

My phrasing is enchanting,
I diction each word clear,
Like a prayer I place it panting
Into the listening ear.

There are some, for instance Maymie,
Who've told me many a time
The folks who heard me claim me
McCormack in his prime.

II

But the taste of folks is changing,
They want the livelier song,
Prefer a wild arranging
Which, to my mind, is wrong.

When thoughts of God and mother
Are lost in the field of art
Our love for one another
Dies in the vacant heart.

Festivals by the dozen
In town, these years, increase,
With everyone's aunt and cousin
Invited to sing a piece.

Though some were good, you bet me
No one exactly cheered;
But me, they won't even let me
Sing when I volunteered.

My voice is as rich as ever,
Richer, in fact, I know,—

Still, in spite of all endeavor,
I can't get near a show.

My gift is put to trial in
My chest all night and day,
I feel I swallowed a violin
I can't take out and play.

The "Lord of all we bow before"
Into the dust is dinned;
"A depth in my soul" they prized of yore
Is gone with the going wind.

III

So I hie me off to the good lands
That lie in the realm of dreams
To serenade the woodlands,
The birds and the silver streams,

Or, shaving in the morning,
Through lonely hours that pass,
I sing to the guy adorning
The square of the looking-glass.

And lately I hear a calling,
In the heel of the dark it comes,
Over the wide world falling
Like the boom of a billion drums,

"Charlie," it says, "you're wanted
In the Kingdom of the Choirs!"
It's maybe because I'm haunted
With unfulfilled desires!

Yet, sometime, I must answer
With all the soul I got . . .
Pneumonia, smash-up, cancer,
It makes no difference what . . .

I'll bound over moon and mountains,
By suns and the last white star;
I'll fly to the golden fountains
Of all the things that are

Where Our Lord and the Virgin Mary
Will be waiting just for me,
The ghost of a glad canary
Who'll turn the tunes, the key

To the Gate that will open slowly
To Two-song Charlie's claim:
"Mother Machree" and "Holy
God We Praise Thy Name."

PART III

TO THOSE WHO SING OF OUR LADY

One night in my room I was all alone,
And with nothing to dream or do,
I said to Our Lady, who hung on the wall,
"I'll spin out a song for you."

So beating a time with the heels of my boots,
I fashioned a chest-full of notes
As easy and artlessly gathered as those
That come from the thrushes' throats.

And somehow I fancied a hushing of wings
On the rim of a blue paradise,
Then the heavenly people applauding because
In pretense I was wondrously wise.

No fiddler can play
No lancer essay
No traitor betray
My love for you.

No robber can steal
No rose reveal
No heart feel
My love for you.

Woods cannot lumber
Stars number
Nor a dream slumber
My love for you.

No axe can swing
No bell ring
And no bird sing
How I love you.

No liar can lie
No crier cry
And no child sigh
How I love you.

Day cannot noon
Night cannot moon
Nor the desert dune
How I love you.

The winter snows
The wind blows
And God knows
That I love you.

ONE SAD MAY MORNING

One sad May morning I well recall,
When I was a small little lad,
Somebody scolded me roundly
For being so bold and so bad.
So I ran upstairs to Our Lady,
To her shrine that we built for the May,
And she smiled on me sweetly and tenderly,
And she dried all my tears away.

Then I pledged my heart to Our Lady,
And I told her I'd ever be true
To her all alone, and I'd love her more
Than anyone else that I knew.

But I left the shrine of Our Lady
With the passing of years and of days,
And I grew to a man, and I wandered afar
From childhood's beautiful ways.
I lived with the toil and the sorrow
In the towns and the cities of men;
Now I'd give all the honor and gold that I own
Just to be a wee small lad again, . . .
Just to run upstairs to Our Lady,
To her shrine that we built for the May,
And see her so sweetly and tenderly smile
And dry all my tears away.

My name is Michael Ryan
And I've been tryin'
Eight hours a day for eight weeks' time
To write a rime
About her who holds in the hearts of men but a little place
Although she was full of grace.

When all is said and done
He was her Son
And that's enough for any one.

Long ago I was young and bright
And handsome to the sight.
I was neat at songs and dances
And although I never married
I had plenty of chances
And plenty of romances.

But when all is said and done
There's only one woman
And she is the Morning Star;
I wish I knew it sooner.

With feet as heavy as stone
And a voice like a saxophone
Bald head and wrinkled brow
No woman wants me now
Excepting her alone.
My eyes are watery weak
And in every bone a squeak
And a toothless grin
Like the smile of original sin.

Houseless, poor and old,
Maybe this year, at eighty-seven,
With a stride that's strong and bold
I'll pass through my Gate of Heaven
Into my House of Gold.

THE MAIDEN

There is no learning save of her dear eyes
Whose love is morning starlight in a gloom.
There is no other knowledge but that look
Welled in the Secret Wording of her womb.

A man, if he be tortured with a thirst
Dry as the heated desert waste is wide,
Needs but to let her cool and flowering close
Gather his terrible loneliness inside.

A man, if he spend therein his wealth of years
Of hours and moments, days and nights and days,
Will find his squandered nothing housed in gold
When heaven falls about his glad amaze.

Whose fiber, flesh and bone did Wisdom choose
When Wisdom's Heart fell pulsing to her sigh?
Whose blood, by drop on drop, begot the Blood
For a world to take and drink and never die?

One maiden is the bourne of all desire,
The vine who gave His Body to the Vine,
And only they are wise whose dream has touched
Those lips that gave their color to the Wine.

TO MAURA

There was a little girl like you
With eyes as big and bright and true.
She loved to laugh and play and run
The same as you or anyone . . .
O dulcis et pia
Puellula Maria.

And in the April of the year
When all the long lost flowers appear,
An angel came to her one day
And said to put her dolls away . . .
O dulcis et pia
Puellula Maria.

She meekly bowed her dark brown head
To what the blessed angel said,
And, swift as the flying of a dove,
She changed from child to mother love . . .
O dulcis et pia
Puellula Maria.

Thus, as the years go by for you,
You'll change as children all must do;
Love with its burden, love with woe
Will come as it came long, long ago . . .
To *dulcis et pia*
Puellula Maria.

But lest your tender heart be torn
With sorrow's ache and sorrow's thorn,
Teach it to love and ever stand

Close to the touch of the small white hand . . .
Of *dulcis et pia*
Puellula Maria.

And when you're old and gray and lone
She'll come to claim you for her own,
Take you to Heaven out of pain,
Make you a little girl ever again . . .
O dulcis et pia
Puellula Maria.

MÉLODIE IRLANDAISE

I

When I came here from Ireland
A lonely Irish boy,
Shy of my Celtic accent,
Shy of my Celtic joy,

I hired me to a lady,
A lady newly wed,
A young and delicate beauty
With the proudest golden head.

The tones of her cultured speaking,
The phrase of her gentle thought,
Were quick with lights and colors
That never were bred or bought.

Her eyes were sea-blue diamonds
Set soft in a petal face;
Each turn of her slender body
Had a smooth and girlish grace.

The amity she showed me
Was like a bag of bail
To the power of love imprisoned
In the soul of a youthful Gael.

On the grounds of her summer mansion,
Her wide and green estates,
I cut the lawns and hedges,
Repainted rails and gates.

When frost, in the cool of autumn,
Was white on leaf and stone,
She'd go away for the winter
And leave me there alone

With the warden and his missus
Who directed, day by day,
My hundred routine duties
Till she returned in May.

II

When spring came on, I found me
Wanting her return
Like the willows want their verdure,
Like the forestbeds their fern.

She'd greet me with excitement,
Hold out her slim, soft hand,
Ask for my health and comfort
And my mother in Ireland.

She'd pile her hair in a crowning,
Don overalls and blouse,
And work with me in the gardens
That terraced from the house.

She taught me the life of flowers,
Their stigmas, bulbs and tubes,
And smiled at the innocent wonder
Of us Roman Catholic rubes.

Our contact formed a friendship
That eased my homesick pain,

And drew the dry wit from me
And made me gay again.

I found the key to her laughter,
A pure and bubbling well
That sounded above the blossoms
Like notes of a silver bell.

I'd call the iris, Irish,
The magnolia, Mag O'Neil,—
And to feel that I made her merry,
By gob, it was good to feel!

Sometimes, in planting clusters,
She'd bend close to my side,
And the bliss, at her scented nearness,
Was more than I could abide.

As she moved among the jonquils,
The hyacinth and rose,
I vowed no bloom her equal
That from the brown earth grows.

III

She inquired of my religion,
So I told her all I could,
And for one who was half a pagan
She thoroughly understood.

I talked of the Blessed Mother
And of what her dearness meant,—
To every truth I uttered
She seemed to give assent.

And she fetched from her room in the mansion,
With the pride of an eager girl,
A tiny bronze Madonna
Wrapped in a golden curl.

'Twas a toy she bought in Milan
When she was but a child,
And hidden among her keepsakes
Was Our Lady meek and mild.

At her behest, in the garden
We made a secret shrine
That shed a winsome meaning
On bower, plant and vine.

IV

Her husband was a creature,—
Athletic, handsome, grand,—
But he took her so for granted,
It was hard to understand.

The cook, and Flo, the laundress,
Declared him good enough,—
Yet, something sly about him
Made me brand him half a bluff.

They were seldom alone together,
For his glee it was to greet
Droves of company he needed
To make his life complete.

Nights, in July or August,
They'd hold a supper dance

I read on her costly tombstone
Her life's brief summary—
And found, to my consternation,
She was nine years older than me.

"God grant you peace!" I murmured,
Kneeling me down to pray
A rosary of sorrows
For the darling who passed away.

At a spot I thought the nearest
To her heart beneath the mound,
I pressed a Lady Medal
Deep in the dewy ground.

I rose, as I slowly blessed me
With the Cross's sacred sign—
And a song through my soul went singing,
"Now that she's dead, she's mine!"

I

We are the American soldiers
At rest in the Arms of God.
Our bodies sleep in an alien sea,
Or under an alien sod.

We left our homes, securest
Of homes in all the world,
To follow our flags of freedom
Wherever they were unfurled.

Ours was the cross of soldiers,
To act, nor question why—
Steep in the straights of duty
To suffer and to die.

We know now why we perished,
And what they killed us for,
A vision veiled from sly eyes
Who pawn in the games of war.

They do not guess our secret
Who stand in the halls of state
By the paper earth they arrow
To mark the tribes they hate.

Isled in the springs of pardon,
We quell our blame for them
Who move, on lands and oceans,
Their blights of stratagem.

As our souls of pride and passion
Were purchased back from hell,
We plead divine forbearance
To their wretchedness as well.

The gentle calm of mercy,
Yes, even they will feel
In the rainbow after the bomb-burst,
In the lull of the storms of steel.

II

But the aim of our attention
Is where our comrades grieve,
The hidden henchmen toiling
In the fight we had to leave.

The burden of our pity
Is for our wounded friends,
Shattered, crippled, blinded,
In their night that never ends.

The toll of our compassion
Is for the aching fears
Our going caused our loved ones,
The heartbreak and the tears.

O blood of our blood we squandered,
Look up in hope, we pray,
To the towers of our many mansions
In the blaze of Eternal Day!

Far as the blowing breezes,
Free as the wind we wing

In the glory of our childhood
And the throning of Our King.

We who were slain for our people,
We who were sacrificed,
Come to the Body of Our Lord
To kiss the wounds of Christ.

The streaming fire of His loving,
Fierce in its agony,
Drives in our naked spirits
A lance of ecstasy.

Through Him we reach Our Father
Whose images we bear,
Whose torrents of Omnipotence
Sustain our strength to share.

Through Him we have Our Paraclete,
Whose Holiness we hold
As a petal guards a perfume,
As a snowflake keeps the cold.

III

When the clocks of time were stricken,
As we were stricken, mute,
We heard the step of the small foot
That crushed the crawling brute.

When Justice flew to find us,
In the van of the Kingdom Come,
We saw His soft Reflection
In the glass of a Speculum.

The touch of her sunbeam fingers
Only the dead man knows
When his ghost is held to the bosom
Of the Sinners' Last Repose.

"Ave Maria!" we murmured,
The wording came somehow
Instinctive as a fledgling
Finds notes upon a bough.

She hears, and the Gate of Eden,
The single Key and Lock,
Opens wide in a welcome
To her latest lonely flock.

She leans on us her longing,
The blossoms of her grace
That swirl as flights of polar fleece
On the anguish of embrace.

She nestles us in counsel;
She whispers, and her breath
Lumes with lamps of firmaments
The sable night of death.

Where are the scribes who hide her
From the yearning hours of youth
Athirst for the milk of Our Mother
Whose breasts are sweet with Truth?

What is the lore of masters,
The smothering sift of sand

That trapped our gaze from the Princess
Who rules our Promised Land?

Who lost the Woman God built,
The only course He made
That passages to Paradise
From valleys in the glade?

Above the stab of the doubter,
The suave and reasonless,
Now she is ours in a knowing
Too real for a proof to press.

Beyond the pale of the liar,
Beyond the close of fame,
Out of the bounds of darkness
That plunges after flame,

The dearness of a Maiden
In her radiant cloak of noon,
Her diadem of diamonds
And her slippers of the moon,

Stands, and her tendernesses,
Like a surge of summers, flow,
Flooding depths and fathoms
In our wanting someone so.

IV

Tall as the tops of mountains,
Terrible as suns,
The armies of her angels
Look on us little ones.

126

Clear in her courts of music
These mighty motives churn
With pictured pride and pleasure
That deep in our beings burn.

The swelling rain of their chanting
Soaks in the trembling ground
A harmony of thunders
Choired to a bloom of sound.

Before Our Lady's splendor
The array of their lines deploys,
Dimmed, in their pluming planets,
To the leaden lists of toys.

The billions of our colleagues
March down upon us then
To clasp us in the triumph
Of the strict salute of men:

Joseph, John and Peter,
Magdalene, Patrick, Joan,
Who chose in our breathing battles
Of intellect and bone—

With these, our clan, our kindred,
The heroes of our race,
Used to the fold of fingers
And the curved caress of a face,

We hail the Queen of Heaven
In her robe that humans wear,

The Majesty of Mary
Crowned with her golden hair.

v

Beloved of the living,
We well remembering dead
Discern the thoughts you're thinking
And the puzzles in your head.

We understand your questing,
Who spoke your native names:
Will there be bags of popcorn?
Will there be baseball games?

Will there be trees in Heaven,
With silver on their leaves?
Cottages full of candlelight,
And ivy on the eaves?

The scent of lavender gardens.
In the cool of fountain mist?
Borders of Easter lilies
That bumblebees have kissed?

Romances by a hearth flare?
The merry cheer of wine?
And grapes upon the branches
When the branches meet the Vine?

Will there be health and heather,
And mornings on a hill?
A lake to fish, a plane to fly,
And the strong delight of skill?

Will afternoons be roaring
In a multicolored bowl
When the sleek and cleated victors
Plough a pathway to the goal?

Will there be ice cream sodas?
A primary grade coquette,
Whose crisp and fragrant innocence
A memory won't forget?

Will dread disease be done for,
And pain be gone for good?
Fatigue and sorrow finished,
And each one understood?

Will folks be bland and gentle,
Gracious, mild and brave?
Will bitterness be vanquished
In the life beyond the grave?

And the history in stories
Thrilling down a scanted page,
Will it all be reenacted
Like a play upon a stage?

Will there be turkey dinners?
And a family picnic drive?
A pool for fun and laughter,
And the tingling when you dive?

Will the men be fair and charming,
And the women bonny, true?

Will there be old-fashioned dances
In the ballrooms of the blue?

Will there be design, chromatics,
Perspective, tone and form?
A thoroughbred to saddle,
And a sail that rides the storm?

Will there be Christmas bundles—
A doll, a ring, a gown?
And the glint of iris evening
On a tiny harbor town?

Will the found or lost battalions,
Supreme or hindermost,
All regiments of nations,
Join to a single host?

Will the miracle of brotherhood,
Gloomed in the crime of Cain,
Glow in the level grandeur
Of the flowers on the plain?

Will our fathers and our mothers
Who perished in their prime,
Our sisters, sons and daughters
Gone in their tuliptime,

Some lilac maids of laughter
Who played along our street,
Some bantling lads of mischief
Stilled by a strange defeat,

Will they shout to us and run to us,
And take us to the core?
And will we love and know them
As we never knew before?

VI

O darlings, valed in hours,
On your errant earth exiled,
Eye hath not seen nor ear heard
Nor heart conceived the wild

Intensity that drowns us—
Supernal, Infinite,
Too great for power to utter
A simple stone of it.

Magnified by millions,
The pleasures worlds afford
Are straws of the harvest gathered
In the gleaning of the Lord.

We cannot tell you everything,
But this much we can speak:
When your hopes are burned to ashes,
And courage falters weak,

Kneel at a Lady Altar,
And bend your weary mind
On the lentil Lap of Wisdom
For the comfort you will find.

When doctrine tears to tatters,
Her soft, explaining words

Will come to cote inside you
Like eager-homing birds.

She'll exegete the mystery
Of the way Our Saviour went,
The why of His Cleansing Waters,
The Blood of His Sacrament.

She'll praise your cross, your challenge,
The pick with which you mine
A treasure when she takes you
Signed with its sacred sign.

She is the need of the traveler,
Guide of a destined road,
The trail through tangled forests
To the Trinity's Abode.

Our Father set her station,
Omniscient His decree,
No one or thing beside her,
But always only she.

Ah, we who own her beauty,
We want to creep around
Beneath the waving waters,
Beneath the rolling ground,

To where our corpses slumber,
With her medals and her chains
To bind as hers forever
The poor dust of our remains!

Hear our young voices calling,
Singing from afar
The prophecy of springtime,
The song of the morning star.

For us all shades are shattered
That glazed the eternal plan,
From the dark of the first creation
To the Light of the God-made-Man.

The total clears to a focus
Of meaning and reward,
Or the anguished woe of motherlands,
Or the drop of red on a sword.

The stripes that veined with crimson
Our uniforms of flesh
Line to the constellations
That gleam on an azure mesh.

Higher than falcons soaring
In the sportive mirth of a boy,
We laugh at the torturing trials
Turned to a sweep of joy.

We glee in the jeweled gladness
Foretold by moons of pearl,
The lark on the lip of the sunrise,
The rose on the mouth of a girl.

In our minds is the full of Knowledge,
In our wills the full of Love:

Safe in a nest, the eagle,
Warm in a nest, the dove.

Now we are one with the Oneness
Of the Sigh, the Son, the Sire,
In the happy end of journey,
In the term of all desire.

We wait beside the portals,
We watch at Heaven's Gate,
O dearest, for your coming
With all our lives we wait.

Glory to Our Creator,
To His Redeeming Word,
And to Our Sanctifier
Be hymns of glory heard!

Though our bodies sleep in alien seas,
Or under an alien sod,
We are the American soldiers
At rest in the Arms of God.

Finis